CANADA

New Hampsnire

Vermont

Maine

Massachusetts

Rhode Island

Connecticut

New Jersey

Delaware

Maryland

New York

Pennsylvania

Washington, D.C.

Wisconsin

Michigan

Minnesota

Iowa

Illinois

Indiana

Ohio

West Virginia

Virginia

Missouri

Kentucky

North Carolina

Tennessee

South Carolina

Arkansas

Mississippi

Alabama

Georgia

Louisiana

Florida

N

W

E

S

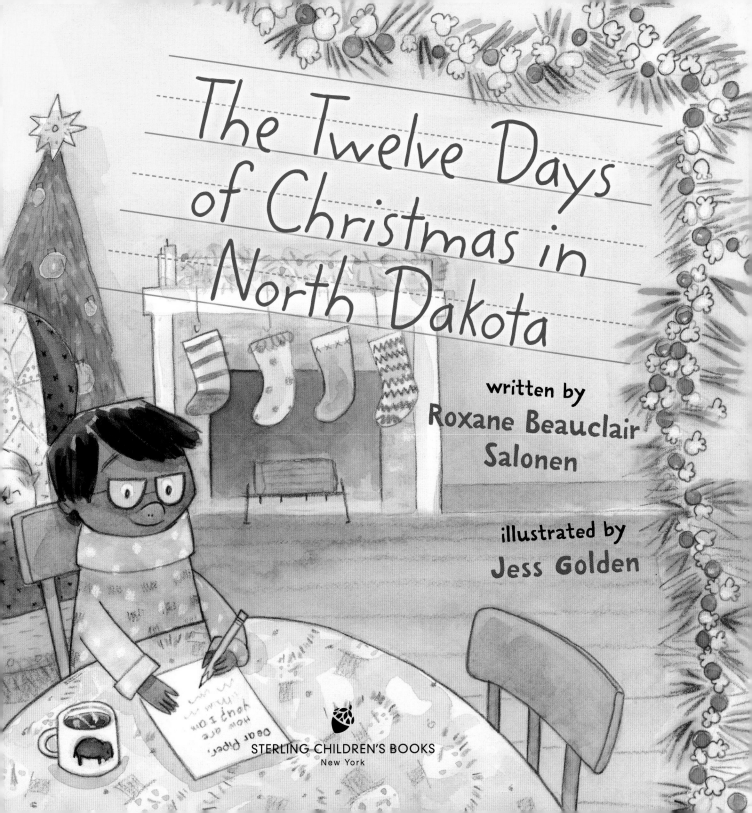

The Twelve Days of Christmas in North Dakota

written by
Roxane Beauclair Salonen

illustrated by
Jess Golden

STERLING CHILDREN'S BOOKS
New York

Dear Piper,

Are you ready to explore the North Pole with me? North Dakota—emphasis on *north*—might be the closest we'll get to the real thing, but I promise, this adventure will be every bit as cool.

Mom has some earmuffs and gloves waiting for you. Our state has gotten as chilly as -60 degrees Fahrenheit before (Brrrr!), in February 1936—the same year we set a record of 121 degrees in July. But don't worry. We're good at staying warm, and we're also the sunniest state along the Canadian border, so pack your shades.

We'll start out here in Bismarck, but we'll be dancing our way through the state, especially when we visit some relatives at Standing Rock Reservation for a wacipi, or powwow. Standing Rock is home to the Hunkpapa and Sihasapa Lakota, along with the Yanktonai Nakota. Did you know that "Lakota" means "friends"? You're going to make a lot of new friends on your trip here!

In addition to all the dancing, get your taste buds ready to be dazzled. And don't expect much down time. You're going to have so much fun here on the prairie!

Your eager-to-see-you cousin,
Henry

Dear Mom and Dad,

Would an American elm tree fit in our yard? It's the North Dakota state tree, and to welcome me to Bismarck, Henry gave me one! It can grow to 100 feet tall, with a trunk as wide as four feet. Mine came with a real Western meadowlark, the state bird. I named him Marty; he's quite a character.

After some hot chocolate, Uncle George and Auntie Anne brought us to the Dakota Zoo. I loved the timber wolves and their haunting howling, the peacocks' colorful tails, and the peppy prairie dogs—they cracked us all up.

Speaking of funny, on our train ride around the zoo, one of the camels actually spit on Henry. Maybe he was just jealous of Henry's candy cane?

Turns out Marty is quite the fashion plate. I wonder what hat he'll wear tomorrow.

Tipping my hat to you for now,

Piper

P.S. The "Skyscraper of the Prairie"—the state capitol building—was amazing to see. The first capitol, which burned down on December 28, 1930, was much shorter. This one stood out, though, dressed like a giant Christmas tree just in time for the holidays.

Dear Mom and Dad,

Whoa! Today, we saw the world's largest Holstein cow, New Salem Sue. She's 38 feet high and 50 feet long. Sue's not real—she's made of six tons of reinforced fiberglass—but she looked pretty awesome with those jingle bells around her ankles. And now I know where the milk in our cocoa yesterday came from—Sue's real Holstein friends. Moo!

We also stopped at Knife River Indian Villages at Stanton, where we saw a replica of the earth lodge where Sakakawea would have lived. She is the Lemhi Shoshone woman who guided Lewis and Clark on their trip west. The buffalo blanket looked cozy, but like it might be kind of itchy.

Henry says tomorrow's adventure will be extra colorful, but that's all he'll tell me. Guess I'll find out soon enough.

Got milk? The white drink is "udderly" plentiful here in North Dakota!

Your cocoa-loving kid,

Piper

P.S. We also drove around a huge man-made lake, Lake Sakakawea, to reach our final destination, Garrison, the state's official "Christmas capital." There, we stepped back in time at the Dickens Village Festival, where Marty indulged in a little too much fruitcake. I had to carry him the rest of the way.

On the second day of Christmas, my cousin gave to me . . .

2 Holstein horns

and a meadowlark in an elm tree.

Hey Ma and Pa,

Today, we got to taste what life was like in 1851. The Fort Union Trading Post, a partially reconstructed fort that sits between Montana and North Dakota, once served as a bustling trade center—kind of like our modern-day shopping malls. A Metis-dressed guide showed us replicas of a bull boat, which had its tail still attached, along with a real cannon, tipis, blankets, tools, and cookware.

At the end of our visit, Henry gave me a pair of beaded earrings and a beaded necklace. Now I see what he meant about color. The Lakota definitely have a tradition of creating beautiful crafts.

Too bad the Missouri River was frozen—we could have sailed home on it. Maybe we can come back this summer and give it a whirl?

Love from your sparkling little lady,

Piper

P.S. We're in the middle of oil country. North Dakota has had a history of oil booms, the most recent of which caused the state to have the highest population spike in the country. It's pretty crazy to think those prehistoric plants and other ancient remnants are still helping us thrive.

Frosted Greetings!

Assumption Abbey was in its winter glory today with its snow-speckled spires jutting up toward the sky. I was curious what real monks look like. Turns out they are pretty much like everyone else. The brothers here in Richardton don't just sit around and pray all day. They also stay busy making crafts and handmade products to help the abbey flourish.

In the abbey gift shop, Tah'tae accidentally tasted some of the soap, probably thinking it was candy. Oops! Uncle George bought me a couple of my favorite scented soap bars—prairie sage and chokecherry. While we shopped, we could hear the organist practicing for Christmas services in the church.

Times like these, I miss you both lots, but I wouldn't give up this trip on the prairie for anything.

Joy to the world,

Piper

P.S. Tah'tae recovered from the soap mishap during dinner in the abbey dining room, where we all got to taste homemade sausage and sauerkraut, a popular dish around here thanks to the Germans from Russia who brought their favorite foods to North Dakota. Oh, and the strudel was pretty tasty, too!

"You ever been to Fargo? Yah, sure, you betcha!"

People don't really talk like that here, but we had fun pretending we were "Fargoans" today. Uncle George's farmer friend, Mack, took us Downtown, which sparkled with glimmering Christmas lights and decorations. At the historic Fargo Theatre, we heard the Mighty Wurlitzer organ and watched "A Charlie Brown Christmas."

Along with popcorn, Mack gave me a special gift—a package holding the state's top crop seeds: wheat, hay, sunflowers, soybeans, and barley. Wish I could see these golden seeds blooming in summertime. (I'm planting ideas for later.) With all the food it produces, North Dakota really is a breadbasket for the world.

Later, we went to the Edgewood Golf Course sledding hill near the Red River, which borders Minnesota. Henry and I raced to the bottom. Guess who won? Some hot apple cider ended the day on a warm note.

Tomorrow, we're flying to the pretty city of Medora, so I need my beauty rest. Catch you on the other side of the "Badlands."

Yours,

Piper

P.S. Speaking of flying, guess who visited the Fargo Air Museum today on his "sleigh" (it was really a helicopter)? Yep, Jolly Old Saint Nick himself!

On the fifth day of Christmas,
my cousin gave to me . . .

5 golden seeds

4 scented soaps, 3 bright beads, 2 Holstein horns,
and a meadowlark in an elm tree.

Howdy All!

Today, we saw the incredible Badlands of North Dakota, which are anything but bad. These sharply eroded, natural rock creations, which began forming 80 million years ago, are a meeting of a huge inland sea and volcanic activity. The resulting colorful layers left us all breathless. Add a theatrical stage and some cowboys and cowgirls to the scene and you have the Medora Musical!

It's the off-season now, but some of the cowboys who perform in this popular summer production presented a special Christmas show in the heart of the city this afternoon. Their crooning and heel-kicking really got Marty excited! Afterward, we slurped down pork and beans and chomped on chuck roast at an old-fashioned barbecue. Delish!

Uncle George's plane is about to leave so I'd better drop this in the mailbox, but say hello to Gus the Iguana for me. He'd love it here—in July, at least.

Ready for takeoff!
Piper with the pipes (vocal, that is)

P.S. We met some other, non-singing cowboys today from Killdeer, a popular spot for rodeo enthusiasts. One of them claimed he's the national bucking-bronco champion. I wouldn't want to be that horse!

On the sixth day of Christmas,
my cousin gave to me . . .

6 cowboys crooning

5 golden seeds, 4 scented soaps, 3 bright beads,
2 Holstein horns, and a meadowlark in an elm tree.

Greetings from the tundra!

We spent most of the day ice-fishing on Devils Lake. I didn't spot one devil—it's way too cold—but saw plenty of walleye and perch. Despite the lake's frozen surface, underneath slippery, shiny swimmers flourish in the warm waters. And North Dakotans love their winter fishing! They just hop on their snowmobiles, zoom across the ice, auger down through the layers, set up their poles in the holes, and wait for the striker bell to zing.

I couldn't believe all the people out there! It was like a little city on ice. Uncle George says it was nothing compared to how many people show up for the Devils Lake annual ice-fishing contest in January.

Tonight, Henry and I get to sleep in a fish house. Don't worry, Mom—I've got my thermal underwear and wool socks to keep me toasty!

Your ice princess,

Piper

P.S. This afternoon, we warmed up at the Opera House in nearby New Rockford, where we watched "A Christmas Carol." Auntie Anne calls it "culture in the country."

Hi Mom and Dad,

Today, while visiting Uncle George's Lakota family at Standing Rock reservation, we watched and also got to be part of an actual wacipi, complete with a drumming circle and fancy dancers, who wore colorful feathers, beads, buckskins, and bells.

When Uncle George joined in on the war song, I felt a tingle go down my spine. He sure did look different in his regalia and braids. I've never seen Uncle George so serious.

Afterward, he was joking around again at the feast. The dried deer-meat stew tasted yummy, but I got seconds on wojapi, or chokecherry soup, and fry bread with butter and honey. Super yum! Marty got a little sticky.

Mom, can you give Snickers an extra doggy treat from me? Hanging around this big, warm family has me missing all of you, but I wouldn't trade this experience for all the snowflakes in North Dakota.

I can still feel the drums beating,

Your Piper

P.S. We stopped by Sitting Bull's gravesite today. My heart hurt hearing Uncle George share about his life, which ended tragically here. But I'm proud to be connected to this tribe. Not every family can claim a real hero among them.

On the eighth day of Christmas, my cousin gave to me . . .

8 drummers drumming

7 walleye wriggling, **6** cowboys crooning, **5** golden seeds,
4 scented soaps, **3** bright beads, **2** Holstein horns,
and a meadowlark in an elm tree.

Hello Buff-fellows!

Real bison really do roam in North Dakota. Although only one in 10 million are albino, one of these graces the grounds at Frontier Village in Jamestown, "Buffalo City." I saw it today, but happily heeded the sign near the pasture warning us to keep a distance. Those beasts are big.

I did cozy up to the World's Largest Buffalo, however. The stucco and concrete bison statue weighs nearly 60 tons and stands 26 feet tall. I'm sure glad buffalo didn't end up extinct. They're not only stunning to see but they taste great, too. Uncle George stopped by with a box of buffalo burgers, and Mom, they're both lean and scrumptious—I think you'd like them!

Did either of you know Jamestown once vied to be the capital of North Dakota? That's a coin toss I wouldn't have wanted to lose!

Well, off to search for some buffalo berries. Later!

Piper

P.S. From 1913–38, the U.S. Mint produced a copper buffalo, or Indian Head, nickel. Henry says people still dig them up every once in a while. Think there'd be any in our yard?

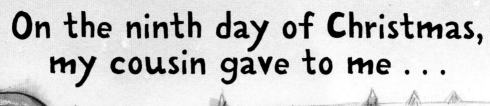

On the ninth day of Christmas, my cousin gave to me . . .

9 bison basking

8 drummers drumming,
7 walleye wriggling,
6 cowboys crooning,
5 golden seeds,
4 scented soaps, 3 bright beads,
2 Holstein horns,
and a meadowlark in an elm tree.

"Velkommen!"

You'll hear this lots in Minot, and why not? We just missed the Norsk Høstfest, North America's largest Scandinavian festival, which the city hosts annually. We did catch the Høstfest spirit gazing at the Dala Horse, waterfall, and Gol Stave Church at Scandinavian Heritage Park.

My sweet tooth burst awake when Henry's friend Jens showed up with some of his grandma's favorite treats, including a delicious Scandinavian pudding called Rommegrot; a Norwegian waffle cookie, krumkake; and lefse, a Norwegian flatbread rolled in butter and sugar.

Jens read us some traditional folk tales about trolls. He says they're not real, but I'm certain I caught one of the troll "dolls" snarling at Marty, who'd tried pulling out some of its shaggy troll hair.

Tonight, we're going to watch a Norwegian Sweater Dance on stage. Sweaters dancing? We'll see.

More soon,

Piper

P.S. I've noticed North Dakota has a lot of modern windmills, called wind turbines. Henry says they convert kinetic energy from wind into electrical power to help keep lights lit. They were popularized by the Dutch, but the Persians invented them.

On the tenth day of Christmas, my cousin gave to me . . .

10 plops of pudding

9 bison basking, **8** drummers drumming, **7** walleye wriggling,
6 cowboys crooning, **5** golden seeds, **4** scented soaps, **3** bright beads,
2 Holstein horns, and a meadowlark in an elm tree.

What's red, green, brown, and tastes delicious? Not a chocolate Christmas tree. A North Dakota pheasant slow-cooked in creamy mushroom sauce and served over wild rice!

We spent today at the Tewaukon National Wildlife Refuge. Dad, I see what you were saying about "big sky." It's wide enough to offer a habitat to a huge variety of waterfowl, shorebirds, wading birds, and songbirds (Marty fits right in). Thanks to some local landowners who wanted to preserve all this wildlife, our feathered friends can now flap happily in the 8,343 acres of native prairie, restored grasslands, and wetlands. Hunters from all over come here to hunt, although you can only hunt deer and pheasants at the refuge.

I sure have a new appreciation for what some people dismiss as "fly-over" country. They're missing out!

Pheasantly yours,

Piper

P.S. Auntie Anne told me that archaeologists recently discovered a new dinosaur near here. The Dakotaraptor, which means "plunderer of Dakota," had long arms, feathers, and a large, sickle claw on its second toe, which could kill relatively large plant-eating dinosaurs. I'm sure glad I live now and not when this thing was flapping its wings around!

Hang on to your seats, I mean skates!

I get now why Dad's so wild about hockey. Watching it up close is crazy fun. That flying puck zooms like a hummingbird on ice, and wham, the players! Can you say body contact?

Uncle George smiled every inch of the flight to Grand Forks, where we watched the University of North Dakota hockey team, his favorite, whop the Northern Colorado Bears 5–0.

Marty didn't like the UND mascot, the Fighting Hawk, at first. But by the end of the game, his "small-bird-syndrome" had disappeared, and he was fluttering around with glee.

My throat hurts from all the yelling, though, so Auntie Anne is making me a warm lemon and honey concoction to drink before bed. She says I'll be back in working order by the time the airplane hits the landing strip back home. But for now, no more caroling.

Getting ready to sip and sleep.

Your pooped-out pixie,
Piper

P.S. When we flew over the Turtle Mountains today, I saw your faces in the shadows below. I'm going to super-duper miss Henry and the gang, but I'm thinking it's time to come home.

On the twelfth day of Christmas, my cousin gave to me . . .

12 skates a-sliding

11 pheasants flying, 10 plops of pudding, 9 bison basking,
8 drummers drumming, 7 walleye wriggling, 6 cowboys crooning,
5 golden seeds, 4 scented soaps, 3 bright beads,
2 Holstein horns, and a meadowlark in an elm tree.

-a-Slant Indian Village

Lewis & Clark Interpretive Center

Washburn

Louise Erdrich *Ojibwe Author*

RISON DAM

Angie Dickinson

Actress

FARGO Film Festival

Largest
then Dam
n the
World

STANDING ROCK SIOUX TRIBE JULY 1873

Lawrence Welk

1903-1992

Big Band Leader & Host

HOTEL DONALDSON

Phil Jackson

BASKETBALL LEGEND

NORTH DAKOTA STATE FAIR MINOT, JULY

Vee

American op Singer 1960's Teen Idol

The Peace Garden State

ON BRICK CO Since 1904

LAKOTA DRIED MEAT (PaPa Soup)

Ingredients

1/2 pound dried meat (beef, buffalo, deer or elk)
4 cups water
1 cup dried corn
1 cup dried sliced tinpsila (prairie turnip)
1/2 onion

Directions: The night before, soak the corn and tinpsila. Add water, dried meat, corn, tinpsila, and onions to a large pot. Whisk over low heat until thick. Cook slowly over the fire for 2 hours until the tinpsila is soft.

North Dakota: The Peace Garden State

Capital: Bismarck · **State abbreviation:** ND · **Largest city:** Fargo · **State bird:** the Western meadowlark · **State flower:** the wild prairie rose · **State tree:** the American elm · **State insect:** the ladybug · **State fossil:** Teredo petrified wood · **State horse:** the Nokota · **State fish:** the Northern pike · **State Latin motto:** *Serit ut alteri saeclo* ("One sows for the benefit of another age")

Some Famous North Dakotans:

Elizabeth Bodine (1898–1986), of Velva, was an American humanitarian and mother of 18. In 1968, she was named Mother of the Year for both the state and the nation. Bodine assisted Native Americans in need, contributed clothing and food to relatives in Poland during World War II, and sent boxes of clothing to Vietnam during the Vietnam War.

Dr. Anne H. Carlsen (1915–2002) was born without hands and feet, but her sharp intellect helped her achieve her doctorate degree and receive international honors for her work with the disabled. She taught in Fargo at a school for disabled children and later became superintendent of a school in Jamestown for the disabled, eventually named the Anne Carlsen Center.

Warren Christopher (1925–2011), a native of Scranton, served as the U.S. Deputy Secretary of State from 1977 to 1981, during which time he led negotiations for the release of 52 American hostages in Iran, spearheaded the normalization of relations with China, and headed the first interagency group on human rights. President Jimmy Carter awarded him the Presidential Medal of Freedom on January 16, 1981.

Ronald N. Davies (1904–1996), after attending high school and college in Grand Forks, went on to work as a federal judge. In that role, he ordered the integration of a public high school in Little Rock, Arkansas, in September 1957—a ruling *The New York Times* called a "landmark decision on racial integration in our nation."

Phyllis Frelich (1944–2014), who was born deaf in Devils Lake, dreamed as a child of becoming an actress, and, as an adult, was one of the founding members of the National Theater of the Deaf. In 1980, Frelich won a Tony Award for the most outstanding performance by an actress for her role in the play *Children of a Lesser God*.

Major General Eldon (Al) Joersz (1944–) is an American pilot who jointly holds the World Air Speed Record, set on July 28, 1976. At that time, he and his co-pilot reached the speed of 2,193 mph, breaking the previously held record of 2,070 mph.

Master Sergeant Woodrow Wilson Keeble (1917–1982), "Woody," was the first full-blooded Dakota Native American (Sisseton-Wahpeton Oyate) to receive the Medal of Honor, the nation's highest military award, for having been treated for over 80 shrapnel wounds one day and returning to duty the next. He once proclaimed, "Fear did not make a coward out of me."

Era Bell Thompson (1905–1986) was an international editor for *Ebony* magazine. A noted journalist, she also authored several books, including *American Daughter*, which details her childhood in North Dakota.

In memory of my grandmother Elizabeth Foster Byrne, who, on Dec. 28, 1930, at age 16,
watched the first capitol burn down, and 85 years later to the day, at age 101, left this world.

For my mother, Jane Beauclair, whose love of children and North Dakota helped get me here, along with my only sister,
Camille Harvey, my best first editor; and for Troy and our children, Christian, Olivia, Elizabeth, Adam and Nicholas,
who've helped fashion some of my favorite memories of this great state.—R.B.S.

For Wyatt—J.G.

ACKNOWLEDGMENTS

In addition to my North-Dakota-loving friends on Facebook who shared their many memories, I want to thank Lindsay Schott,
North Dakota archivist, for her generous input. Additionally, I am indebted to the North Dakota Heritage Center & State Museum,
which provided an incredibly rich environment for all things North Dakota.—R.B.S.

Special thanks to Robyn Baker for her cultural advice and guidance with regard to this book.

STERLING CHILDREN'S BOOKS
New York

An Imprint of Sterling Publishing Co., Inc.
1166 Avenue of the Americas
New York, NY 10036

ISBN 978-1-4549-2008-3

Distributed in Canada by Sterling Publishing Co., Inc.
c/o Canadian Manda Group, 664 Annette Street
Toronto, Ontario, Canada M6S 2C8
Distributed in the United Kingdom by GMC Distribution Services
Castle Place, 166 High Street, Lewes, East Sussex, England BN7 1XU
Distributed in Australia by NewSouth Books
45 Beach Street, Coogee, NSW 2034, Australia

For information about custom editions, special sales, and premium and corporate purchases,
please contact Sterling Special Sales at 800-805-5489 or specialsales@sterlingpublishing.com.

Manufactured in China
Lot #:
2 4 6 8 10 9 7 5 3 1
07/17

www.sterlingpublishing.com

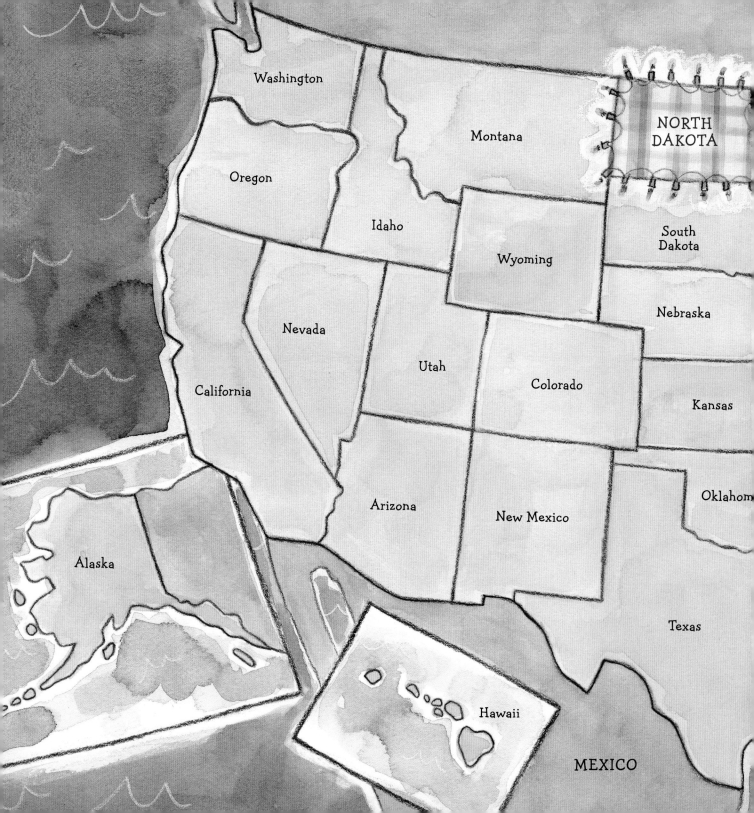